The Months of the Year

...in the Northern Hemisphere

Helena A. Fournier

Ravenhill Books

Library of Congress Control Number: 2023921296
ISBN: 979-8-9890220-5-2

To all dreamers, both big and small,
who heed the seasons' tender call…

January

January welcomes a brand new year.
Sparkling winter fun is here!
Children make angels in the snow,
their smiling faces all aglow.

February

February snowflakes flurry along
a winter wind howling its final song.
Little sprouts hide beneath the snow,
promising flowers are soon to grow.

March

March winds blow winter away.
Kites circle in the sky each windy day.
Green is the color that starts to appear
now that spring is finally here!

April

April weather likes to joke and play
just like we do on April Fool's Day.
A day in April could have either rain or sun
and sometimes they mix for some rainbow fun!

May

May is filled with spring's enticing tunes
of birds singing softly in the afternoons.
Apple tree blossoms float in the air,
it is the time of the year that is lush and fair.

June

June is the month of balmy nights
that cover the meadows in dewdrop delights.
With midsummer dreams of strawberry cake,
children go berry picking when they awake.

July

July sun can be smoldering hot,
but ice cream and lemonade help a lot.
Bike rides, county fairs, and water play,
relax on a porch swing after a fun-filled day.

August

August air tastes warm and sweet
from peaches and plums ripe in the heat.
Hazy sunlight and golden trees
are mellow whispers of the autumn breeze.

September

September Harvest Moon shines bright
over fields and orchards in the night.
Crispy winds swirl around
as autumn leaves fall on the ground.

October

October leaves raked into piles,
children jump in with great big smiles.
A pumpkin patch and a fun corn maze,
these are the best of autumn days.

CORN MAZE

November

November mornings are frosty and cold
as winter begins to take hold.
Playful winds make branches sway
blowing the last autumn leaves away.

December

December brings in holiday joy
of old traditions we honor and enjoy.
On Winter Solstice, the longest of nights,
we brighten our homes with candle lights.

Now that the months are crystal clear,
let's move on to the seasons of the year!

Through the *Four* Seasons

Winter is the season of icy delights,
of stars that shine brightly in the nights,
and of frosty clouds, and heavy snow
that gently falls on Earth below.

In *Spring,* life sprouts anew everywhere!
Playful winds spread pollen in the air.
Sunshine mixed with spring showers
fill the meadows with colorful flowers.

Summer is the season of long, lush nights
when fireflies shine their whimsical lights.
The days are filled with warmth and sun,
swimming, playing, and lots of fun.

In the *Fall,* the air starts cooling down,
the leaves turn yellow, red, and brown.
We revel in pumpkins and apple cider,
exciting corn mazes, and wonky spiders.

Test your knowledge
by drawing a line from each month to its season.

August

May

January

November

June

December

March

July

October

April

February

September

Fall

Winter

Spring

Summer

www.ingramcontent.com/pod-product-compliance
Lightning Source LLC
Chambersburg PA
CBHW041539260326
41914CB00015B/1500